SHREK TALES

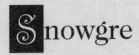

Snowgre

By Michael Anthony Steele

Scholastic Inc.

New York   Toronto   London   Auckland   Sydney

Mexico City   New Delhi   Hong Kong   Buenos Aires

ISBN: 0-439-59717-X

Published by Scholastic Inc.
SCHOLASTIC and associated logos are trademarks and/or registered trademarks of Scholastic Inc.

12 11 10 9 8 7 6 5 4 3 2   4 5 6 7 8/0

Designed by John Daly
Printed in the U.S.A.
First printing, October 2004

Fwop!

Shrek plunged his hand into the mud. "Gotcha!" he yelled as he tightened his grip on his prey. Then Shrek yanked his fist out of the bog with a loud *shhhlop!*

Smelly slime dripped from his green hand as Shrek held his prize. The small swamp toad dangled between two of the ogre's thick fingers. He compared the toad to the two others he had in his pocket. It wasn't much bigger, but it would have to do.

Shrek walked back to his cabin. As his hollow-stump home came into view, he glanced toward the trail leading out of his swamp. Coming over the hill was a thin man wearing a brown jerkin and pushing a wooden handcart. Even though he was far away, Shrek could see the man struggling with a huge package strapped to the cart. Shrek shook his head and trudged toward his cabin.

Since he had rescued Fiona in front of the entire city of Duloc, he didn't seem to be as scary to everyone. People from town no longer walked miles out of their way to avoid his swamp. Even the fairy-tale creatures visited him with annoying frequency. As Shrek neared his home, he decided to make an example of the approaching man. He would wait inside his cabin, and when the guy was close enough, Shrek would swing open the door and scare him within an inch of his life. Shrek smiled at the thought.

With a little chuckle, the giant ogre dashed inside his cabin and slammed the door behind him. With his back to the door, he waited to hear the man's footsteps.

"Well?" Fiona asked him. She was stirring a large, bubbling pot over the fire. Wisps of putrid steam rose from the concoction.

Startled, Shrek suddenly remembered why he went out in the first place. He fumbled through his pockets and pulled out the three tiny swamp toads. He held them up with pride.

Fiona stepped closer to her husband. She leaned in to examine the tiny toads dangling between Shrek's green fingertips. "They're not really big enough for a casserole," she said. "Maybe they can garnish my toad-stool stew."

"Uh," Shrek stammered, "this isn't really a good time of year for swamp toads." He quickly put one of the toads to his lips and blew into its mouth. The toad expanded like a green, slimy balloon. Shrek clamped his fingers on the toad's mouth to keep the air in. "See," said Shrek with a smile, "it's bigger."

Fiona laughed and shook her head.

"I told you," said Donkey. He sat in a chair beside a front window. "You two should be vegetarians like me. It's always a good time of year to be a vegetarian."

"Oh, it is, is it?" Shrek asked. "Well, what about wintertime?"

Donkey thought for a moment. "Oh, yeah," he said. "Winter's not really good for us vegetarians." Donkey stretched his head out the window and bit the top off a flowering thistle weed.

"Donkey!" Fiona yelled. "My flowers!"

"Uh-oh," said Donkey with a full mouth. "I forgot." He poked his nose out the window and spit out the weed. He cocked his head to one side. "Hey, Shrek, are you expecting company?"

"What?" asked Shrek.

There was a timid knock on the front door.

The approaching man! Shrek dropped the toads and grabbed the doorknob. Two of the toads hit the ground and escaped under the door. The inflated toad sputtered around the room like a deflating balloon. It zipped out the window.

Preparing to roar, Shrek took a deep breath and swung open the door. He only gasped, however, when a scroll and quill were thrust toward his face.

"P-p-p-please sign for the d-d-delivery, sir," the man stammered. He quivered nervously from the top of his brown jerkin to the bottom of his brown tights.

Shrek let out his breath in a sigh and angrily snatched the parchment away from him. Maybe after he signed, he would scare the life out of the little man.

The ogre scribbled his name on the scroll, handed it back, and glanced at Fiona. "Are you expecting a delivery?"

"No," she replied. "My SmellCo Stain Improver isn't due for another week."

Shrek glanced back at the doorway. The man was running full speed up the trail, pushing the empty handcart ahead of him.

Shrek stepped outside. Beside the door was a large package taller and wider than the ogre himself. It was wrapped in brown paper and covered with several damp stains as if it had sprung a leak. Fiona and Donkey joined him outside.

"What'd you get? What'd you get?" Donkey asked excitedly. He jumped in front of Shrek to get a better look.

"I don't know," Shrek said as he casually picked up Donkey by the ears and tail and moved him aside. Then he reached up and tore away some of the damp paper. He was surprised to see that there was no box underneath. Instead, the entire package was a huge block of ice.

"Ice?" Donkey cocked his head. "What did you order ice for? You're an ogre, not a polar bear. You making smoothies or something? I love smoothies!"

Shrek cupped his hands to his face and peered into the block of ice. He stepped back. "Oh, no!" he cried. "Not him!" The ogre stormed back into his cabin.

"Him?" Fiona looked at the ice. "There's a 'him' in there?"

"There's a 'him' all right," Shrek called out. He plopped into his chair and crossed his arms. "And 'him' is not staying!"

"Nonsense," said Fiona. "Whomever it is, we can't leave him frozen like this." She pushed up her sleeves and crouched behind the enormous block of ice. With a small grunt, Fiona picked up the huge block and carried it inside.

Donkey's mouth hung open as he watched Fiona's display of ogrely strength. "Uh . . . I'd help you with that but my old football injury has been acting up lately." He followed her inside. "Never make her angry," he muttered, reminding himself. "Never make her angry!"

Fiona put down the block of ice beside the fireplace. She tore off the rest of the paper and then threw another log on the fire.

Donkey clip-clopped up to the block and peered inside. "Hey, there *is* someone in there."

"It's my cousin," Shrek announced grumpily. "He's a snow ogre named Snowgre. He's from the land Far Up North." Shrek shook his head. "They think being frozen in a block of ice is the best way to travel."

"It doesn't sound too dumb to me," Donkey said as he examined the frozen ogre. "It beats waiting in line at those carriage security checkpoints."

"If he's family, why did you want to leave him outside?" asked Fiona. She grabbed the poker and stoked the fire. Beads of water ran down the sides of the ice.

"Because the last time he showed up," Shrek growled, "he was nothing but trouble."

"Well, tell us what happened," said Fiona.

Donkey trotted closer. "Yeah, Shrek. Tell us a story!"

Shrek sighed. "All right." He pushed his chair close to the fire and pulled another chair closer for Fiona. Donkey sat on the floor between them. "But when I'm done," Shrek continued, "you'll want to chuck his block of ice into the swamp, too!"

Many years ago, before Shrek knew Donkey or Fiona, he lived happily in his swamp. He was content to live alone, dine on slugs, and bathe in his smelly bog. Occasionally, he had to frighten away pesky, torch-carrying villagers. But then again, that was more fun than a chore. Life, he thought, was very good.

Then one day, as Shrek sat down to eat a small rack of weed-rat kabobs, he heard a knock at the door. A bit irritated, Shrek got up from his table to answer. Surely it wasn't one of the villagers. None of them were brave enough to actually come up to his cabin, much less knock on the door. Nevertheless, he took a deep breath, ready to give one of his finest roars.

Shrek swung open the door to see someone he hadn't seen in many years — his distant cousin Snowgre. Arms wide, the large ogre grinned from ear to ear. He looked much like Shrek himself except he was taller, fatter, and covered in thick white fur.

"Cousin Shrek!" greeted Snowgre. "It's been far too long!"

Before Shrek could reply, Snowgre gave him a great big hug. "Hey now," Shrek uttered nervously. "Okay, that's enough."

"I would have gotten here sooner, but I decided to skip the ice block and take the scenic route." Snowgre let go of Shrek and stepped past him into the cabin. He looked around the sparse dwelling. "So, this is where you're living now."

Annoyed, Shrek closed the door behind him. "By all means, come in."

"Thanks," Snowgre replied. He took off his heavy coat and threw it onto the bed.

"What do you want?" Shrek asked.

"That's the first thing you ask your long-lost cousin?" Snowgre retorted. "That's extremely rude, you know." He continued to inspect Shrek's cabin. "Can't a family member pay another family member a visit sometime?"

Shrek picked up Snowgre's coat and opened the front door. "Not when one of them wants to be left alone."

Snowgre laughed and slapped Shrek on the back. "That's what I love about you, Shrek — always joking." He continued his inspection tour of Shrek's home.

Shrek sighed and closed the door.

Snowgre strode to the table and picked up one of the weed-rat kabobs. "I'm sure you'd ask me to join you for supper. But I see you barely have enough for your-self." Snowgre took a bite from the weed rat and grimaced as he chewed. "A little bland."

"Hey, that's my dinner!" Shrek yelled.

"If you want to call it that," Snowgre said with a smirk. He dropped the kabob back onto the plate. Then he reached into his coat pocket and removed a rather large block of moldy cheese. "Lucky for me, I brought my own."

The cheese had a putrid aroma so harsh it curled Shrek's nose hairs. But to an ogre, it smelled absolutely delicious.

Snowgre ripped off a hunk of cheese and offered it to his cousin. "Now this is what *I* call dinner."

Shrek took a bite of the stinky cheese. It tasted as good as it smelled. He had eaten weed rat for the past three nights, so the moldy cheese was a nice change. "Where did you get such a big hunk of cheese?" Shrek asked.

"Big?" Snowgre laughed. "This is nothing. I ripped this off a block of cheese as big as your house."

Shrek chuckled between chews. "Sure you did."

"It's true," Snowgre assured him. "You should see where I live now. It's a grand castle, high on a mountaintop." He took another bite and swallowed. "I dine on only the finest foods, like any self-respecting ogre should."

"Hey," Shrek sputtered. "There's nothing wrong with the way I live."

"Oh, sure," Snowgre replied. He pointed at the puny weed-rat kabob. "If you like that sort of thing." He strolled to the window. "Where do you bathe? Let me guess, some dreary old mud pit?"

"It's not a mud pit," Shrek growled. "It's a bog."

Snowgre laughed. "Why bathe in a bog, my boy, when you can soak in the finest sulfur springs? It's wonderful for the sinuses." He snapped his fingers. "I have a great idea. Why don't you come for a visit?" Snowgre threw an arm around Shrek's shoulders. "I've seen where you live. It's only proper that I return the favor."

Shrek wasn't sure. He looked over at the puny rats on his table. Weed rat was one of his favorite foods, but after eating some of his cousin's cheese, it didn't seem as appetizing. Shrek then looked down at Snowgre's big belly. He could be telling the truth. His cousin looked far from underfed.

"All right," Shrek replied. "I'll come."

"I can't believe you left your swamp so easily," Fiona said as she put another log on the fire. Snowgre's block of ice had melted so the top of his head was now exposed. His small, furry ears protruded from each side.

"Well, I was younger then and less set in my ways," Shrek admitted.

"What was Snowgre's place like?" Donkey asked. "Was it everything he said it was?"

"Yes and no," Shrek replied.

S nowgre led Shrek to the land Far Up North. Pine trees stretched toward the sky and snow-covered mountains surrounded them. Shrek brushed some of the fallen snow from his coat as Snowgre led him to the base of one of the mountains.

Snowgre pointed to the mountain. "From here, it's straight up."

This mountain was so tall that Shrek couldn't see its peak. Its rocky face reached skyward and disappeared into a cloudbank. Shrek pulled his thin coat tighter as he followed his cousin up the slope.

The two ogres climbed for several minutes until they found themselves surrounded by giant sulfur pits on a large plateau. The pungent steam rising from the bubbling pits added to the surrounding clouds, reeking of rotten eggs.

Snowgre halted his climb and began taking off his clothes.

He's crazy, Shrek thought. *All this bone-chilling wind has frozen his brain.*

Snowgre stripped down to his underwear and ran toward a sulfur pit the size of a small lake. He stepped off a nearby boulder and leaped high over the bubbling pit. At the last second, he pulled his body tight, forming a cannonball dive. Molten sulfur splashed all over Shrek.

"What are you doing?" Shrek shouted.

Snowgre poked his head out of the liquid. "We're almost there." He splashed about. "I just thought you'd want to relax in a nice hot bath after the long trip."

Shrek looked around. He was a bit sore from the long journey, and his body felt like a big, green snow cone. Plus, the festering stench of heated sulfur was very appealing.

"Oh, what the heck," he agreed, beginning to remove his clothes. When he was down to his underwear, Shrek stepped over to the pit and dipped a big toe into the bubbling sulfur. The liquid was boiling hot. It would have stripped the hide off any man or beast. However, it was just right for an ogre. With a sigh of delight, Shrek slowly slipped into the giant pit.

"What do you think, Cousin?" asked Snowgre.

Shrek stretched his arms over the lip of the bubbling pool. "Not bad," he replied. "Not bad at all."

Shrek closed his eyes as the hot sulfur churned around his body. He hated to admit it, but Snowgre was right. A soak like this was far more relaxing than one in his bog back home. He could get used to this.

Suddenly, the ground began to shake. Rocks and small boulders dislodged from the mountainside and rolled downhill. Snowgre immediately climbed out of the giant pit.

"Okay, time's up," Snowgre announced. He grabbed his pile of clothes and moved away from the pit.

"What are you talking about?" Shrek asked. His eyes were still closed, and a peaceful grin stretched across his face. "I'm just starting to feel my toes again."

Snowgre dried off his face. "Shrek, you have to get out now." The ground shook even harder.

"Get out?" Shrek's eyes were still closed. "Not after you turned on that great vibrating action."

"I didn't make anything vibrate," Snowgre yelled over the rumbling. "Get out now!"

Shrek opened his eyes and saw a scared expression on Snowgre's face. Then he looked around and saw the boulders rolling downhill. The rumbling grew more deafening.

"Now, Shrek!" Snowgre yelled. "Get out NOW!"

Shrek scrambled out just in time. The pit exploded behind him. It spewed a column of steam and boiling liquid as wide as the giant pit itself. It sounded like a freight train as the pillar of molten sulfur shot high into the sky. If Shrek had remained inside, he would have been shot over the mountaintop.

The pit continued to spew for almost a full minute before finally dwindling back to its original form. Once again, it steamed and bubbled peacefully.

Standing in his underwear, dripping wet, and shivering from the cold, Shrek glared at Snowgre. His cousin was almost dressed and didn't seem bothered by the eruption at all.

Snowgre smiled as he put on his heavy coat. "Well," he said, "now that we're both relaxed, we can finish our journey." He threw his scarf around his neck and proceeded up the mountain.

Shrek took a deep breath to calm his pounding heart. He had never felt less relaxed in his entire life.

After getting dressed, Shrek followed Snowgre up the steep slope. They climbed over jagged rocks, trudged through deep snowdrifts, and skidded atop large patches of ice. After Shrek could no longer feel his fingertips, Snowgre stopped and pointed to a giant castle made of snow and ice. Even from a distance, the castle looked much larger than Shrek expected. Its towers stretched high into the clouds and its walls seemed to wrap around the mountaintop.

"There it is," Snowgre announced. "Home sweet home."

Irritated by the sulfur pit incident and the freezing climb, Shrek didn't want to give him the satisfaction of being impressed. "Nice igloo," he said sarcastically.

"It's not an igloo," Snowgre corrected. He looked shocked that his cousin would think such a thing. "It's a glorious castle!"

"Is it made out of snow and ice?" Shrek asked.

"Well, yes," Snowgre admitted.

"Then it's an igloo," Shrek said.

Snowgre was speechless as Shrek trudged past him. After a few steps, Shrek allowed himself a small chuckle.

When the two ogres reached the castle, they crossed its huge drawbridge and walked toward its two massive front doors. The doors themselves were made out of giant redwood trees. Shrek was looking around for some way to push the immense doors open when Snowgre grabbed his arm.

"Uh . . ." Snowgre stammered, "those are out of order."

Shrek followed him along the side wall of the cas-tle until they reached a large crack. Snowgre slipped through and Shrek followed him.

They emerged inside a gigantic hallway. The walls reached so high, Shrek could barely see the ceiling. Dusty cobwebs stretched across enormously oversized furniture. A thin layer of sludge covered the floor and icy slime oozed from the walls. Shrek hated to admit it, but Snowgre was right. This castle was quite grand!

"Are you hungry?" Snowgre asked. "Maybe you'd like a nice appetizer before dinner."

"Sure," Shrek replied as he scanned the amazing castle interior.

"This way," Snowgre directed. He entered a small opening at the bottom of the adjoining wall. Once in-side the wall, Snowgre grabbed a nearby torch and scraped the tip along the ground. The torch ignited like a match and he held it high over his head. Its light revealed a long, winding staircase. The steps looked as if they were made with giant ice cubes.

Shrek followed his cousin up the icy stairs. They ducked under some huge pipes and jumped over some large cracks until they reached another opening. They stepped through and found themselves on what appeared to be an oversize kitchen counter. To Shrek's surprise, he saw a humongous block of moldy cheese. It sat on a giant cutting board next to a giant knife. Snowgre was right — this cheese was nearly as big as his cabin in the swamp.

"What did I tell you, Cousin?" Snowgre asked.

"That is one big hunk of cheese," Shrek admitted.

Snowgre bent down and picked up the large knife. Using both hands, he swung the blade toward the cheese and sliced off a large chunk. Then he broke it in two and offered half to Shrek.

Shrek took a big bite and closed his eyes. The cheese must have grown moldier while Snowgre was away. It was positively delicious.

Shrek opened his eyes to see that Snowgre wasn't

enjoying his bit of cheese. Instead, the snow ogre glanced around nervously.

"What's the matter?" Shrek asked.

Snowgre shushed him. "Did you hear something?"

Shrek was about to ask what he was supposed to be listening for when a huge bony paw reached over the top of the cheese block. Its sharp claws dug into the cheese as another paw appeared beside it. The beast climbed on top, revealing itself to be a giant rat. But this was no ordinary rat. It had bushy fur and two long, sharp teeth. It was a giant, saber-toothed snow rat!

"Stop! Stop!" Donkey cried. He pulled his long ears down with his front hooves. "Don't say another word!" He sprang to his hooves and dove under Shrek's bed. "I don't want to hear how you and Snowgre got eaten by that giant snow rat!" Only the front half of his body fit under the bed. His rear end stuck out.

"But, Donkey —" Shrek began.

"No way!" Donkey shouted. His hind hooves scraped the floor as he tried to crawl completely under the bed. "I don't want to hear how he grabbed you with his nasty rat paws . . ."

"Donkey," said Fiona.

". . . and how he chewed you into little bits with his nasty rat teeth!" he continued.

Fiona walked over to the bed. "May I ask you a question, Donkey?"

The entire bed shook as Donkey trembled beneath it. "Okay," he whispered.

"If the big rat ate Shrek and Snowgre," she asked, "how could they be here right now?"

For a moment, there was no answer. Then the bed stopped shaking. Donkey poked his head out and gave Fiona a big smile. "You know, that's a very good point." He scampered out from under the bed and trotted back toward the fire. "Sorry, Shrek," he said, pulling himself together. "I got a little carried away. It must have been your master storytelling. Yeah, that's what it was. Your riveting dialogue and expert use of descriptive adverbs captured my imagination and —"

"*Anyway*," Shrek interrupted. He tapped Snowgre's block of ice. "My cousin here didn't see the rat right away. He just heard it nibbling on the other side of the cheese. . . ."

Snowgre looked up just as the rat leaped onto the counter. Before Snowgre could move, the rat swiped at him with one of its long claws. He dropped his cheese, tripped over the knife, and tumbled off the countertop. Luckily, Snowgre caught the edge with one hand and didn't fall to the floor below.

As the rat scuttled toward Snowgre, Shrek raised his block of cheese over his head. "You want some cheese?" he shouted. "Here you go!" Shrek flung the large block. The cheese struck the rat in the head, knocking it over.

While the beast was down, Shrek ran to the edge and grabbed Snowgre's arm. He quickly hoisted his cousin to safety. Then, with Snowgre in the lead, they both ran across the counter.

The rat scrambled to its feet and chased them. The two ogres dashed for the hole, but they weren't going to make it. The huge rat was gaining fast.

Shrek glanced over his shoulder and saw the rat pounce. The ogre leaped into the air at the same time. He landed on one end of the knife as it lay across Snowgre's dropped hunk of cheese. Like a teeter-totter, the handle of the knife shot up and hit the rat square in the belly. It launched the beast across the enormous kitchen.

Shrek ran into the hole to find Snowgre standing just inside. "What kind . . . of place . . . is this?" Shrek exclaimed, panting. "Every time I begin to enjoy my-self, it's 'Get out of there, Shrek' or 'Don't get eaten by the giant rat, Shrek.'"

Snowgre nudged Shrek with his elbow. "It beats

the puny weed rats back in your swamp, eh, Cousin?"
He laughed nervously.

"At least *I'm* the one who eats the weed rats!" Shrek
yelled. "Not the other way around."

Snowgre laughed again and slapped Shrek on the
back. "Come on. All that exercise has given me an appetite. Let's go eat."

As Shrek followed Snowgre down the passageway,
he let out a big sigh. For this he had left the warmth
and comfort of his swamp?

The two ogres traveled inside the wall until they came to another set of stairs. They quietly descended until they reached another dark opening. Snowgre stepped right through, but Shrek was a bit hesitant. There was no telling what he would find in the next room.

"Come on, Cousin," Snowgre yelled. "You're going to love this."

Shrek sighed, shook his head, and moved toward the opening. As he stepped through, he balled his hands into fists, just in case.

They stood in the first normal-sized room Shrek had seen yet. However, the room's size didn't grab his attention. Mouth agape, he stared at what was *inside*.

The room was filled with vast amounts of everything an ogre would ever want to eat. Racks of giant slugs hung from one wall. Each one was as tall as Shrek himself. There were massive jars full of large eyeballs, huge squirming grubs, enormous clattering beetles, and pickled penguin beaks. Shrek saw more blocks of stinky cheese and giant loaves of moldy bread. A steaming pile of fresh walrus blubber filled one corner of the room. After the rat fight, Shrek had briefly lost his appetite. Now he was so hungry, his mouth watered. He wiped it dry with his shirtsleeve.

Snowgre laughed at Shrek's look of amazement. "What did I tell you, Cousin?"

"I had my doubts," Shrek replied, "but this is impressive." Then he glanced over his shoulder. "There aren't any more saber-toothed rats, are there?"

"No, not in here," Snowgre assured him.

Shrek put his hands on his hips and leaned forward. "Nothing is about to explode, is it?"

Snowgre chuckled. "Not this time."

Shrek smiled and clapped his hands together. "Then let's eat!"

The two cousins enjoyed a wonderful feast — ogre style! While Snowgre slurped down some tasty grubs, Shrek made himself three hefty slug-and-cheese sandwiches. They both spread eyeball jelly over hunks of bread, garnished with dusty cobwebs for that extra zing of flavor. Then they washed down their dinners with two helpings each of beetle juice.

After eating all they could, Shrek and Snowgre sat on the floor in a corner of the room. Shrek smiled as he rubbed his full belly. He hadn't eaten that much in a long time. For the first time during his visit, not only was Shrek not freezing, but he was glad he had come.

Suddenly, the wall Shrek sat against swung away from the rest of the room. He had to catch himself to keep from falling backward. Shrek stood and stared in disbelief as an enormous hand reached into the room and grabbed the jar of beetles. The giant hand removed the jar from the room and then pushed the wall back into place.

Shrek turned to face his cousin.

Snowgre just shrugged and kept eating.

"Oh, I get it!" Donkey said. "That was a *giant's* hand."

Shrek nodded. "That's right."

"And Snowgre lived in a giant's ice castle," Fiona added.

"You guessed it," Shrek confirmed. He stood and walked over to Snowgre's block of ice. Now only a thin, frozen wall surrounded his cousin. "Snowgre lived there just like a little mouse."

"That would explain a lot," said Fiona. "Like the giant rooms and the giant rat."

Donkey grimaced. "Man, I didn't know giants eat the same nasty stuff ogres eat."

"You'd be surprised," Shrek informed him. "They're the ones who grind people's bones to make bread, remember?"

Donkey crinkled his nose. "Now that's disgusting."

"So what did you do?" asked Fiona.

Shrek grabbed the fireplace poker and stirred the burning embers. "Well, as you can imagine, I wasn't very happy."

Wait, Shrek," Snowgre pleaded as he followed his cousin down the winding staircase. "There's nothing to worry about."

Shrek whirled around. "Nothing to worry about?" he roared. "You live in a castle with a giant. A *giant's* castle!" He turned and continued down the stairs.

"It's not a bad relationship," said Snowgre. "There's plenty of room, we like the same foods . . ."

Shrek turned back to him again. "You're a pest, like a mouse or a cockroach! You're lucky the giant hasn't called the exterminator."

Snowgre folded his arms. "Well, deciding who is the pest in this castle really depends on how you look at the situation," he explained. "Besides, you have to admit that living here is much better than staying in that dreary swamp of yours."

"You mean my dreary, *warm* swamp?" Shrek asked. Now he was fuming. "Listen, you," he said, poking Snowgre in the chest. "I'd rather eat my puny weed rats in peace than dine on fine foods and worry about being stepped on!"

Shrek began to leave once more but Snowgre grabbed his arm. "All right, you can go," he said. "But before you do, let me show you one more thing."

"Why?" Shrek asked. "What could you possibly impress me with this time?" He shook off Snowgre's hand. "You know what would impress me right now? A heater! A campfire! Something! It's bloody cold!"

"I don't want to impress you anymore," Snowgre said. "I just want to show you one thing."

"Then I can go home?" Shrek crossed his arms. "Back to my swamp?"

"Absolutely," Snowgre agreed.

"All right, but make it fast," Shrek demanded. "I've had all the luxurious living I can stomach for one day."

Snowgre lit another giant matchstick torch and led them down another corridor and up a different set of stairs. This time, when they emerged from the hole in the wall (which was just a big mouse hole), they found themselves in what appeared to be the giant's living room. A huge couch sat in front of an enormous fireplace. A smaller, but equally oversize table stood against the opposite wall.

Snowgre blew out the match and pointed to the

table. Shrek peered at it and saw a metal cage sitting on top.

"It's a cage," said Shrek. "What about it?"

"Look who's inside," Snowgre instructed.

Shrek squinted his eyes and saw that there *was* someone inside. After staring a bit longer, he realized that a female snow ogre was trapped there. She was a little smaller than Snowgre, had the same white fur, and had long blond hair.

"That," said Snowgre, "is my wife, Snowflake." He hung his head. "That's why I brought you here. I need help rescuing her."

SEVEN

"That's so sweet," said Fiona. She put an arm around Shrek's shoulder. "He had to rescue her just like you rescued me."

"That *is* pretty romantic, Shrek," Donkey chimed in.

"Romantic, nothing," Shrek growled. "He tricked me into going there with him."

"Would you have helped him if he had just asked?" Donkey inquired.

"Probably not," Shrek replied. "But that's not the point, is it? It's the principle of the matter."

Fiona hugged him tighter. "You would've helped him, and you know it," she said. "You're always a hero."

Shrek gave a sheepish grin as his green cheeks turned red. Then his smile vanished and he squirmed out of Fiona's hug. "Well, I wasn't feeling very *heroic* that day, I can tell you."

You tricked me!" Shrek yelled at his cousin.

Snowgre shushed him and glanced around nervously. "Please, keep your voice down."

"I don't care!" Shrek shouted even louder. "You lied and dragged me away from my cozy swamp — where I don't feel like I'm turning into a frozen Shreksicle!"

"I know," Snowgre admitted. "And I'm very sorry. But I didn't know what else to do." He hung his head. "I can't rescue Snowflake by myself."

"Well, you could've told me," said Shrek.

"You're absolutely right," Snowgre agreed. "But I'm telling you now, and I desperately need your help."

Shrek didn't answer. He turned his back to his cousin.

"I'm begging you." Snowgre knelt on one knee. "Do this one thing before you leave."

Shrek remained silent.

"Please?" Snowgre pleaded.

Shrek sighed and shook his head. "Fine," he said reluctantly.

Snowgre hopped to his feet. "Wonderful," he cried. "I always knew you had a good heart."

"Oh, yeah?" Shrek growled. "Well, when I get back, I'm going to see a doctor and have it removed!"

"You won't regret this, Cousin," Snowgre added. "Now, we just need a plan."

"No plans. No more talk," Shrek barked. "Let's get this over with." He strode out into the room.

Snowgre remained by the wall. "But there's one more thing I have to tell you."

Shrek didn't slow down. "I don't want to hear it."

Fuming, Shrek stomped toward the giant table. He

couldn't believe his cousin would trick him like that. In fact, the more he thought about it, the angrier he became. Shrek was so irate that he could feel his heavy footsteps vibrate the floor below. They vibrated hard . . . too hard.

Puzzled, Shrek slowed down a bit. The vibrations only grew stronger. His stomping wasn't causing them — it was something else. Shrek looked to see what it was just as a giant hand reached for him. Before he could get away, two huge fingers lifted him off the ground by the back of his shirt. They belonged to a little boy. A *giant* little boy.

"Put me down!" Shrek shouted.

The giant boy didn't answer. Instead, he held Shrek close to his face. From the tiny ogre's point of view, the boy's brown hair looked like a tangled forest. Each freckle on his nose was the size of a huge pancake. Hunks of food as big as loaves of bread were stuck between his crooked teeth.

The boy looked over his shoulder. "Petunia!" he bellowed. "Come see what I found!"

The floor rumbled as the giant boy's sister tromped into the room. Her crooked pigtails flapped wildly as she ran. When she was closer, she knelt to get a better look.

"Goody!" she exclaimed. "Now we *both* have a pet ogre, Trevor!"

Shrek struggled to free himself. "I'm nobody's pet anything!"

Petunia leaned closer to him. "Eww, this is an ugly one!"

"Hey, now," said Shrek. "There's no call for insults."

Back near the wall, Snowgre cupped his hands around his mouth. "That's what I wanted to tell you!" he shouted. "The giant has children!"

"Oh, no!" Donkey cried. "Shrek is going to be trapped in that castle forever!" He leaped to his hooves and ran for the bed again.

Shrek grabbed him by the tail and pulled him backward. Donkey's hoofs scuffled on the floor as he kept running. "Donkey," Shrek assured him, "I'm right here, remember?"

Donkey stopped running. "Oh, yeah," he said with an embarrassed chuckle.

"Shrek," a voice said behind them.

Startled, everyone jumped up. They saw that the ice had completely melted away from Snowgre's furry face.

Donkey put a hoof to his chest. "Don't sneak up on someone like that."

"Sneak up?" Snowgre asked. "I've been standing here the entire time listening to my cousin's exaggerated story."

"Exaggerated?" Shrek asked.

Snowgre smiled at Fiona. "Congratulations on the wedding, by the way. I'd give you a hug, but my arms are still frozen." A thin layer of ice still coated the rest of his body and a large chunk covered his feet.

"It's very nice to meet you," Fiona replied.

"Yeah, I've never met a snow ogre before," Donkey added.

"Hang on a minute." Shrek pushed past Donkey. "What do you mean 'exaggerated'?"

"I mean, dear Cousin, that it wasn't as bad as all that," Snowgre explained.

"Oh, sure," Shrek said sarcastically. "It was quite a vacation. Come visit Snowgre's winter wonderland! If you're not squished by a giant, you may be lucky enough to only freeze your ears off!"

"Well, then forgive me for being rude," Snowgre said in his own sarcastic tone. "Don't let me interrupt your *chilling* yet completely *accurate* tale."

"Yeah, Shrek," Donkey agreed. "Finish the story."

"Tell us how you got away from those giant children," Fiona prodded.

Shrek scowled at Snowgre once more, then turned to Fiona and Donkey. "Well," Shrek began, "I created a diversion while Snowgre rescued Snowflake."

"Ahem!" Snowgre cleared his throat. "Why don't you tell them *how* you created a diversion?"

"Well, uh . . ." Shrek stammered. He scratched the back of his head and glanced away. "Actually, the kids put me in a round glass jar with a cork in it so I couldn't get out."

"Like a snow globe?" Donkey asked. "You were stuck

in there with the Eiffel Tower or something, and then they'd shake it up really hard, and it would snow like a blizzard, and then —"

"No," Shrek interrupted. "It wasn't a snow globe! It was just a round glass ball. That's it."

"Go on," Snowgre urged, "tell them everything."

Embarrassed, Shrek looked down. "Okay, they played with me as the ball rolled around on the floor," he mumbled.

Eyes wide, Donkey and Fiona looked at Shrek and then at each other. They burst into laughter.

"They put you in a hamster ball!" Donkey screamed as he rolled onto his back, cackling loudly.

"I don't think it's very funny!" Shrek growled.

Fiona stopped laughing and patted Shrek on the hand. "Of course not, dear." Then she quickly covered her mouth to keep from laughing harder.

"Anyway," Shrek continued, "it made a great diversion."

The two giant children knelt on either side of Shrek. He was trapped inside the glass ball that rolled along the floor as he walked.

"Roll this way, little ogre!" Petunia yelled.

"No, roll to me! Roll to me!" Trevor cried.

Shrek did neither. Instead, he ran inside the glass ball, and it rolled away from both of them.

"Hey!" Petunia screeched. She quickly stood and sprinted past Shrek, blocking his way. "You have to roll to one of us!" Then Petunia kicked the glass ball toward her brother. Shrek tumbled inside as it sped across the floor.

There were only two good things about this situation. First, all the exercise was keeping Shrek warm. Second, Snowgre was busy rescuing Snowflake. While the humongous kids played with him, Shrek noticed Snowgre climbing the long tablecloth up to her cage.

"Watch this!" Trevor exclaimed. He reached down and gave Shrek's ball a spin. Shrek was plastered to the side of the glass as the ball twirled on the floor.

"I think I'm going to be sick," Shrek gasped.

When the ball came to a stop, Shrek was so dizzy he could barely stand. Petunia jumped up and down. "That was funny! Do it again! Do it again!"

"Oh, no!" Shrek protested. He glanced toward the table. The cage door was open and Snowgre and Snowflake were climbing down the tablecloth. As far as he was concerned, his diversion duties were officially over.

Trevor reached for the ball to give it another spin. Just as he was about to grab it, Shrek threw himself against the side, propelling it away from his grasp. Shrek ran as fast as he could toward the far wall. If he struck it hard enough, maybe the glass ball would break.

"Get back here, you stinky little ogre!" Petunia yelled.

The floor vibrated as the kids chased him. Shrek didn't dare look back. Instead, he ran faster. He was at full speed when he hit the wall. The tremendous force slammed him against the glass. Unfortunately, the ball didn't break.

He stood and grabbed his aching head. "Okay. Plan B."

Shrek ran the opposite direction. The ball rolled away from the wall and toward the approaching children. As they were almost on top of him, he made a sharp left and then a right. He zigzagged through their legs. Trevor slammed into Petunia as the ogre rolled toward an open doorway.

Wham! Thud-thud!

Shrek looked back to see the two children lying in a tangled heap on the ground. "That'll teach you," he said with a laugh.

He was almost at the open doorway, but something didn't look right. There was no floor past the opening. When he was too close to stop, Shrek realized why. The door was at the top of a long, icy staircase.

Clank! Clank! Clank! Clank! Clank!

Shrek tumbled inside the ball as it bounced down

the stairs. Not only were they giant steps, but they seemed to go on forever. Shrek wasn't counting the steps, however. He wasn't even thinking about being tumbled inside the ball. Only one thing was on his mind: *Why won't this ball break?*

Clank! Clank! Clank! Clank! Clank!

He was almost at the bottom of the stairs. The front doors to the castle were just beyond them. Shrek was sure that the ball would break when it struck one of the doors. After all, he was going twice as fast now.

The ball bounced off the bottom step and flew through the air. Shrek braced himself for impact. Unfortunately, he didn't hit the doors. At the last second, they swung open, and in walked the father giant. He was three times the size of his kids and carried a large spiked club. The giant scowled as Shrek flew between his legs and bounced down the drawbridge.

Shrek finally came to a stop in the fluffy snow outside the castle. He stumbled to his feet and saw that the glass ball didn't have a single crack in it. He pushed and kicked at the cork but it wouldn't budge.

Snowgre and Snowflake ran up to the ball. "We did it, Cousin!" Snowgre yelled.

"Yes, thank you very much," said Snowflake.

"Fine," Shrek replied. "No problem." He kicked the cork again. "Now lend a hand and get me out of here!"

Snowgre glanced back at the castle. "I'm afraid there's no time!"

Shrek looked back to see the giant standing in the doorway. His kids were on either side of him.

"Daddy, our pet ogres are escaping!" Petunia screamed.

"Don't let them get away!" yelled Trevor.

Raising his club over his head, the father giant ran toward the ogres. Shrek pushed on the side of the ball. Snowgre and Snowflake were already running down the mountain. He quickly rolled after them.

Shrek bounced down the snowy mountain. He felt the ground shake as the giant chased after him.

Fwooooom!

A nearby snowbank exploded as the giant slammed his mighty club onto the ground.

Fwooooom! Fwaaaaap! Fwooooom!

Shrek pushed the ball left and right as he ran, dodging the giant's blows. Each time, the giant barely missed smashing him.

Snowgre, Snowflake, and Shrek were nearly at the bottom of the mountain. As the giant closed in, Shrek's ball hit a wet patch of snow. A layer of snow coated the outside of the glass ball, turning Shrek's glass ball into a rolling snowball. Shrek could no longer see where he was going. But he felt the glass ball rise as more and more snow packed onto his rolling snowball.

The giant raised his club, ready to pound Shrek into the ground. But instead of swinging his weapon, the giant accidentally stepped on Shrek's large snow-ball. His humongous foot rolled over it and he slipped. The giant stumbled down the mountain slope, and Shrek's ball shot toward a rocky outcropping.

Smash!

The ball hit a sharp rock and shattered around him. Snow and shards of glass flew everywhere. Shrek was finally free.

The giant tumbled, soaring over Snowgre and Snowflake. He landed, face-first, in the huge sulfur pit.

Sploooooooooosh!

Dripping with boiling sulfur, the giant got to his

feet, roaring with rage. But as he stood, the ground began to shake. Before he realized what was happening,
the giant was launched skyward by an erupting column of steam and sulfur.

"Yeeeeeeeeeeeeaaaaaaaaaaaoooooooooooh!" screamed
the giant as he shot toward the mountaintop, disap-
pearing into the clouds.

Snowgre and Snowflake ran toward Shrek as he
shook off a few remaining shards of glass. "Well done,
Cousin," Snowgre congratulated him.

"Yes, that was the best trick I've seen in a long
time," Snowflake agreed.

Snowgre slapped Shrek on the back. "This calls for
a celebration! We'll sneak back inside and have the
biggest feast three ogres have ever had."

"Let's go for a swim first," Snowflake suggested.
"We're already here at the pits."

"So true, my dear," Snowgre agreed. "So true!"

Shrek couldn't believe what he was hearing. They

almost had been clubbed, captured, and squashed. Yet Snowgre and Snowflake acted as if nothing had happened! Were they insane?

"Forget it!" Shrek roared. "I'm going home!"

"But Cousin," said Snowgre, "we have to reward you for all your help."

"Surely you can stay awhile," Snowflake added. "You must enjoy some more of our hospitality."

"I've had enough of your hospitality!" Shrek barked. "I'm going to go home to my simple swamp and eat my simple food. At least there I don't have to worry about being killed or used as the family pet."

Shrek stormed down the mountain.

"And so I came home," Shrek said. "The end." He stood and stretched his legs.

Donkey sighed. "I love a story with a happy ending."

"It was a happy ending, all right," Shrek agreed. "I came back to my swamp away from that madhouse he calls home." Shrek pointed a big, green finger at Snowgre.

Snowgre was almost completely thawed. All that remained of the ice was a small block encasing his feet.

He placed his hands on his hips. "For your information, Cousin, we don't live there anymore."

Shrek raised an eyebrow. "You don't?"

"No, we don't," Snowgre replied. "We moved to an entirely new ice castle."

"A *giant's* ice castle?" Fiona asked.

"Well, of course it's a giant's castle," Snowgre said. "We've grown accustomed to a certain standard of living, you see."

"Oh, of course," said Shrek, shaking his head.

"But these giants are much nicer." Snowgre reached into his coat pocket and pulled out a picture of himself and Snowflake posing with two enormous giants. The two ogres were very tiny in the image and the giants' heads were cropped out of the top. "We all live together in perfect harmony. There's no running or hiding, and they never treat us as pets."

Everyone leaned over and looked at the picture. "Well, good for you," Shrek grumbled.

"They seem very nice," said Fiona politely.

"In fact," Snowgre continued, "that's why I came here. I wish to invite you all over for a visit."

"What?" Shrek jumped behind Snowgre and began to push him toward the front door. The ice block, encasing his feet, slid smoothly on the floor. "No way, nothing doing!" Shrek yelled.

Donkey leaped to his feet and jumped up and down. "Oh, can we go, Shrek? It'll be so much fun! Can we go? Please? Please? Pretty please with sugar on top?"

Shrek stopped and glared at Donkey. "Were you even listening to the story?" he demanded. "Snowgre and his giants are nothing but trouble."

"Yeah, but these are *different* giants," Donkey explained.

"Giants are giants!" Shrek yelled. "They can still squash you like a bug if they don't watch where they step."

Shrek began to push Snowgre again, but Fiona

placed a gentle hand on his shoulder. "These giants don't sound like the other ones. And it would be nice to meet Snowflake."

"Absolutely," Snowgre agreed. "The only thing you have to worry about is their dog."

"Dog?" Fiona asked.

"A *giant* dog?" asked Donkey.

Snowgre waved a dismissive hand. "Oh, Fifi is very sweet." He let out a nervous laugh. "Although she does play rough sometimes."

"That's it!" Shrek yelled as he threw open the door and slid Snowgre outside. "Thanks for visiting." Shrek placed both hands on Snowgre's back. "Come back when you can stay longer." Shrek pushed as hard as he could. The large snow ogre slid smoothly on the block of ice around his feet. "Bye-bye now!"

"Shreeeeeeek!" Snowgre yelled as he skidded down the trail, over the hill, and out of sight.

Shrek closed the door. He hugged Fiona. "For your information, I'm very happy with our simple home."

Fiona squeezed Shrek tightly. "Me, too."

Donkey snuggled his head between them. "Me, three!"

Shrek laughed and playfully pushed Donkey's head away. "You don't live here, Donkey."

Shrek let go of Fiona and grabbed his apron hanging by the fireplace. "How about some barbequed weed rats?" he asked. "I'm grilling!"

"That would be wonderful," said Fiona.

He put on his barbeque apron. KISS THE COOK was written across the front. "Some plain, ordinary, delicious weed rats," he added.

Fiona kissed him and smiled. "I wouldn't have it any other way."

Don't miss:

SHREK 2 Movie Novel

SHREK 2 Movie Storybook

SHREK 2 *Cat Attack!*

and coming soon:

Shrek Tales #3
Open Centipede!